Made in the USA
Monee, IL
21 March 2022

93245752R00057